Sister Magic

Mabel Strikes a Chord

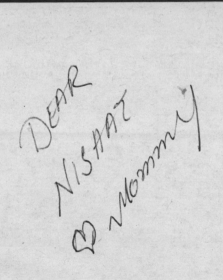

DEAR
NISHAT
♡ Mommy

Sister Magic

Mabel Strikes a Chord

BY ANNE MAZER

ILLUSTRATED BY BILL BROWN

SCHOLASTIC INC.

New York Toronto London Auckland Sydney
Mexico City New Delhi Hong Kong Buenos Aires

To my favorite piano player

No part of this publication may be reproduced, stored in a retrieval system, or transmitted in any form or by any means, electronic, mechanical, photocopying, recording, or otherwise, without written permission of the publisher. For information regarding permission, write to
Scholastic Inc., Attention: Permissions Department,
557 Broadway, New York, NY 10012.

ISBN-13: 978-0-439-87249-2
ISBN-10: 0-439-87249-9

12 11 10 9 8 7 6 5 4 3 2 1   8 9 10 11 12 13/0

Printed in the U.S.A.   40
First printing, July 2008

Chapter One

Plonk, plunk, plank. Violet banged noisily on the electronic piano.

Her older sister Mabel came into the room, holding her hands over her ears. "What is this racket, Violet?"

"I'm making music." Violet flipped a switch on the keyboard. She banged some more.

Strange and terrible sounds floated out.

"Here. Let me show you the *right* way to do it." Mabel sat down next to her little sister on the bench and began to play a march.

Mabel's hands flew over the keys. She had taken piano lessons since first grade.

Now she was in third grade. She could play a march, a waltz, and a dance, and lots of other things, too.

Only last week, her teacher had praised her highly. "Good work, Mabel," she said. "You are making progress."

Mabel loved making progress. She loved doing things the right way.

Violet never wanted to do things the right way. She only wanted to do things *her* way.

When Mabel tried to show her what to do, Violet didn't like it. She scowled at her older sister.

"You always hog the piano," she accused.

"It's called practicing," Mabel explained patiently.

"So?" Violet was in kindergarten. She didn't practice anything. She did whatever she wanted. That didn't include piano lessons.

Mabel played the last few bars of the march. She didn't miss a single note.

When she was done, she turned to her little sister. "See? *That's* real piano playing."

"I like my music," Violet said stubbornly. She began to thump on the piano keys again.

Mabel went over to the bookshelf and took out some sheet music. She glanced at the clock.

"Ten minutes, Violet," she said. "Then it's my turn again."

Mabel still had a couple more pieces to practice. She wanted to get them perfect before her next lesson.

Violet didn't answer. One by one, she pounded on the black keys.

"Those are the sharps and flats," Mabel said in her best teacher voice.

"Sharps? Flats?" Violet repeated in disbelief. "No way."

"Sharps and flats are sounds," Mabel explained.

"You're teasing me."

"Believe it or not, that's what the black keys are called."

"*Keys?*" Violet said, banging extra hard on them. "Pianos don't have doors."

"They're musical keys, silly!" Mabel said in exasperation. "When will you ever learn?"

Violet thumped out a few more horrible sounding chords. Her skinny legs dangled off the edge of the piano bench.

Mabel put her fingers in her ears and waited for her to finish.

Violet crashed and bashed on the piano. Then she turned around. "Did you hear that, Mabel?"

"Yes," Mabel groaned.

"Isn't it beautiful?"

Mabel rolled her eyes. "Yes, Violet. It's beautiful."

Violet got up from the bench and bowed. "Your turn, Mabel! I know how to share."

"You sure do, Violet." Before her little sister could change her mind, Mabel slid onto the piano bench and began to play.

Chapter Two

The girls' father owned a clothing store called Clothes To You.

If Mabel wanted a sweater, she only had to say, "Dad, please bring home a size nine sweater, in soft wool, not too scratchy, ribbed, with a round neck and long sleeves, in robin's egg blue."

And that night, she would find the perfect sweater, wrapped in tissue paper, on her bed.

If only everything were that easy!

Mabel wished she could order a little sister from a store. She knew exactly what she would ask for.

WANTED:

1. One sweet, adorable little sister
2. Must have neat, combed hair; a clean face; and matching clothes
3. Should enjoy beading necklaces, playing lovely tunes on the piano, and getting good grades
4. Also must listen well, cooperate, and follow instructions

Mabel thought about the list. It described her very well.

Unfortunately, it didn't describe Violet at all.

Except maybe for the adorable part. Everyone seemed to find Violet adorable.

Sometimes Mabel did, too — and sometimes she didn't.

When Mabel thought about how different she and Violet were, she wondered if there had been a mix-up. Had she gotten the wrong sister?

And would the right one ever show up?

One day when Mabel came home, maybe she'd find her real, perfect little sister waiting for her.

But there was always Violet.

Wild, messy, loud, unpredictable Violet.

The two sisters were helping their mother before dinner.

Mabel was emptying the silverware rack from the dishwasher.

She sorted the clean silverware into a drawer. She lined up all the spoons. She put the knives and forks in order.

"You are such a help, Mabel," her mother said.

Mabel beamed with pride.

"I'm a help, too," Violet said. She ripped open a bag of baby carrots and threw them on a plate.

"Nice job, Violet," their mother said.

Nice? Mabel glanced at the carrots that Violet had dumped out. Was her mother even looking?

Her fingers itched to arrange the carrots in circles or at least line them up on the plate. If it was her job, *she'd* have done it right.

Mabel shut the silverware drawer. She took a stack of dinner plates from the cupboard and carried them to the dining room table.

At least their parents had one child they could rely on.

I must be such a comfort to them, Mabel thought to herself.

Violet began to count the carrots. "One carrot, two carrot, red carrot, blue carrot," she sang.

"Did you learn that in kindergarten today?" her mother asked.

"I made it up myself," Violet announced.

"How lovely, dear," their mother said.

Tuning them out, Mabel began to set the table.

She placed the dinner plates distances from one another.

She folded napkins into triangles.

She put matching water glasses next to each plate.

Violet continued singing.

"Red carrot, blue carrot, one carrot, two carrot," she sang. "Baby carrots everywhere; carrots flying through the air."

Their mother measured soy sauce and sugar into a cup and hummed along with Violet.

"You're not in tune. . . ." Mabel's voice trailed off. Her eyes widened.

Violet was pointing a finger at the carrots.

"*Violet!*" Mabel hissed under her breath. But she was too late to stop her little sister.

The carrots shook. Their bright orange color faded. Then they turned red, white, and blue, like little rolled-up flags, and flew up from the plate.

They floated along the counter, zoomed back down, and began marching over the sink.

Mabel frantically grabbed at them. She prayed that her mother wouldn't turn around.

She couldn't find out about Violet's magic.

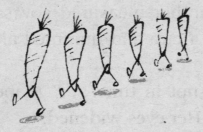

Chapter Three

In the third grade, there were lots of kids with annoying younger sisters.

That was normal.

No one else that Mabel knew, however, had a little sister who turned carrots red, white, and blue.

No one else had an annoying little sister with magic powers.

That *wasn't* normal.

Mabel should have been grateful that Violet didn't make the carrots sing the national anthem.

But she wasn't grateful at all.

She only wished that if Violet had

magic, she would at least learn to use it sensibly.

Like Mabel would have.

If Mabel had magic, she would have used it only for important, practical, serious things.

Like folding her socks perfectly.

Or reading assigned books extra fast.

Or keeping her fingernails extremely clean.

Mabel would never have used her magic in front of her parents, especially not her mother.

Only when everyone was asleep at night would Mabel have flown around the house.

And only if no one was looking would she have changed juice to soda.

Only in the privacy of her room would Mabel have enchanted toys. Or carrots. Or whatever.

Mabel understood how important it was to keep magic secret.

Violet, on the other hand, didn't seem to understand anything at all.

If she did, she wouldn't go around enchanting food right in front of their mother.

What a dumb thing to do, Mabel thought for the hundredth time.

The family was sitting around the table. There was fried chicken, rice, broccoli, and, of course, carrots for dinner.

"Aren't you going to eat your carrots?" her mother asked Mabel.

"No," Mabel said, pushing them to farthest edge of her plate.

"I thought they were your favorites."

Mabel shuddered. Maybe they were. But she couldn't eat something that had just flown around the kitchen.

"You love carrots," her mother said with a puzzled frown. "This isn't like you."

"No, it isn't," Mabel agreed. But the carrots weren't themselves, either.

"*I'm* eating *my* carrots," Violet announced.

"Me, too." Their father helped himself to a large serving.

"Don't, Dad!" Mabel begged.

Her father patted her shoulder. "Calm down, honey. They're just carrots. And they're good for the eyesight."

He crunched down loudly on one. "Mmm, delicious."

Mabel couldn't watch. What would they do once they were in her father's stomach?

"At least eat a couple," her father urged. "You've never been a picky eater, Mabel. Is something wrong?"

Before Mabel could think of a good reply, the doorbell rang.

"I'll get it!" Mabel leaped from her chair.

Saved by the bell. And just in time.

The last time the doorbell had rung during dinner, it had been Uncle Vartan.

At that time, Mabel and Violet had never met him, even though he was their mother's younger brother.

They had barely known that he existed.

Uncle Vartan's visit was a total surprise. No one expected him. No one knew why he had suddenly shown up.

It turned out that Uncle Vartan had magic, too. But before Mabel could ask any questions, he had vanished.

And no one had seen him since.

Her mother refused to talk about him.

Vartan and his magic had made her life miserable, she said. She didn't want to hear about magic ever again.

She didn't want Mabel to talk to her father, either. He didn't know there was magic in the family.

Mabel was on her own.

But if Uncle Vartan came to visit again, she'd ask him all those questions she was dying to ask.

She'd make him explain how magic worked. She'd ask for advice about dealing with her mischievous little sister.

She hoped that he'd give Violet a talking-to.

She hoped that he'd give her a lesson or two in being responsible.

Mabel hoped that she'd see Uncle Vartan on the doorstep now.

Chapter Four

Mabel opened the door wide. But Uncle Vartan wasn't there.

Instead, a burly man in jeans and a T-shirt stood on the porch. He was holding a slip of paper. Behind him was a delivery truck.

"Piano delivery, miss."

"Piano?" Mabel said. "We already have an electronic keyboard."

"I have orders to deliver to this address."

"There must be a mistake."

The man double-checked the delivery slip. "No mistake, miss. Right house, right address, right time."

Mabel didn't believe it. She hadn't heard so much as a whisper from her parents about this.

"No one told me anything."

"You're just a kid. Why should they?"

"You don't understand," Mabel insisted. "My parents tell me *everything*."

The deliveryman sighed.

Mabel's eyes widened as two men unloaded a magnificent piano. "Are you sure it's for us?"

"One hundred percent sure."

Mabel wasn't convinced.

But if her parents hadn't ordered this piano, who had? There was only one other possibility — Violet.

Or, rather, Violet's magic.

* * *

Just a few weeks ago, an Olympic-size swimming pool had appeared in their backyard.

Violet did it all with magic.

The pool was wonderful.

But it had created some very bad moments for Mabel.

The neighbors asked how it had gotten there so fast. They wanted to know who had installed it and how much it had cost.

Mabel's friend Simone wondered about it, too.

Luckily, Mabel's parents hadn't suspected magic at all. Each thought the other had done it.

Mabel felt grateful that Violet had gotten a deliveryman. Like her piano teacher always said, "It's all in the details."

But she wondered why Violet had bothered with a piano at all.

Violet wasn't that interested in music. She just wanted to do what Mabel did.

And as much as Mabel would love a piano like this, she didn't want a magical one.

It would bring up too many questions.

Her parents would want to know who had ordered the piano and who had paid for it.

Simone would wonder why they had both an Olympic-size pool *and* a grand piano.

Mabel could almost see Simone's intelligent eyes gleaming behind her glasses.

She could almost hear her comment: "I thought your family didn't have enough money to go on vacation last year."

What would she say then?

Mabel had to get rid of the grand piano before anyone saw it.

"Excuse me, miss," the deliveryman

said. "I have a crew waiting. We need to bring the piano in now. Get your mother or father, please."

"Um," Mabel said. "Can you wait a minute? I'll get the person in charge."

That was Violet.

The deliveryman wasn't going to be happy when he saw a five year old.

"Hurry up," he said. "I have three more stops to make tonight."

The deliveryman was so . . . *real*. Mabel had to admit that Violet had thought of everything this time.

"I'll be right back," she promised.

But just as she turned to get Violet, her mother showed up.

"Finally," the deliveryman said. "An adult."

"Mom!" Mabel cried. "Stop!"

But her mother had already seen the grand piano. She hurried down the front steps and ran her fingers over the keys.

"Beautiful," she sighed. "Perfect." She nodded to the burly man. "Put it in the sunroom."

"Yes, ma'am," he said. "Right away."

"No," Mabel said.

"Do you think it should go in the living room instead?" her mother asked.

"Don't bring it in the house!"

Her mother stared. "Mabel, what is wrong with you tonight? First the carrots, and now this."

Mabel hung her head. She was still sure Violet had something to do with this.

Her mother was upset. "You're not listening to me, Mabel."

Mabel jumped. Had her mother been talking? She hadn't heard a word of what she just said.

"I told you, your father and I saved up all year!" her mother replied.

"For what?" Mabel asked.

Her mother propped open the door for

the piano deliverymen. "Right in here, please."

Mabel watched helplessly as they brought the piano into the house.

"We bought this grand piano for *you*," her mother said. "We've been planning it forever. At least don't look so miserable about it!"

Mabel caught her breath. For a moment, she couldn't reply.

"You?" she finally squeaked. "Bought a grand piano? For me?"

"Who else? I can't play a note and your father has a tin ear," her mother said. "Violet is too young to care. And you've been practicing so hard. We wanted you to have a real instrument. And then this one practically fell into our hands. What luck!"

"Why didn't you tell me?" Mabel stammered.

"I've been trying to for the last five minutes." Her mother sighed. "Your head is in the clouds tonight, Mabel."

Mabel could scarcely believe her luck. A grand piano — all for her. And it wasn't even magic.

"*Thank* you, Mom!" Mabel threw her arms around her mother.

"That's more like it," her mother said.

Chapter Five

"This is *my* piano," Mabel announced proudly, as the deliverymen brought it into the sunroom.

"So?" Violet said. She stuck out her lower lip.

Mabel knelt down next to Violet. "Now you can use the other one as much as you want," she said.

"So?"

"That will be your very own piano."

"*So?*" Violet said again.

"Put it in that corner," their mother said to the deliverymen.

"Mabel is right," she said to Violet.

Mabel beamed. Those were three of her favorite words.

"The grand piano is for her," her mother repeated. "It's not a toy. It's for a serious student."

Mabel's smile got even bigger.

Violet's frown got even deeper. "*I* want a grand piano like Mabel," she said.

"When you're older, it will be yours, too," their mother said. "You just have to wait."

"But *Mabel* doesn't have to wait!" Violet wailed.

"She's been practicing almost every single day for years," her mother said.

"I can practice, too," Violet insisted.

Their mother shook her head.

Mabel felt sorry for her sister. Well, a *little* bit sorry.

After all, Violet had the magic. Mabel got the grand piano.

Wasn't that fair?

"Will you play one of your songs for me on the electronic keyboard?" she asked Violet instead.

"No," Violet said.

"Please? They're very beautiful."

Violet shook her head.

"I'll teach you how to play 'Heart and Soul.'" Mabel was being very, very nice to her little sister.

But Violet didn't care. She went off in a corner and sulked.

"Leave her alone," her mother said. "She'll forget all about it in five minutes."

"Are you sure?" Mabel asked.

"I know my Violet," her mother said.

The deliveryman brought in the piano bench and set it in front of the piano. "Enjoy," he said.

"Thank you," their mother said. "Do you want to try it out, Mabel?"

Mabel sat down at the grand piano. She took a deep breath. She ran her fingers over the smooth new keys.

She played a brief exercise or two to warm up.

Then she played a few bars of a new song she had just learned.

"Very nice," her mother said.

Her father came into the room and listened, too.

Mabel glanced over at Violet.

She began to play one of her little

sister's favorite songs: "Twinkle, Twinkle, Little Star."

"I hate that song," Violet said.

Mabel switched over to another of Violet's favorites, "When You Wish Upon a Star."

"Ugh," Violet said. She plugged her ears.

"What about this one?" Mabel said. She began to play "When the Saints Go Marching In."

Usually Violet loved that song. Sometimes she marched around the room in time to the music.

But now she only scowled more fiercely than ever.

All right. Be that way, Mabel thought.

She had tried to cheer Violet up. If her little sister wanted to stay in a bad mood, that was *her* problem.

Mabel improvised a little. She played a cascade of notes.

Imagining herself on a brightly lit stage in front of a cheering crowd, she finished the song with a flourish.

"Bravo!" her father called, clapping wildly. "Bravo!"

Mabel got up and bowed.

"That was really good, honey," her mother said.

"It sure was," her father agreed. "My little girl is going to be a concert pianist one day."

Mabel smiled modestly.

Her mother looked thoughtful. "You just gave me an idea, Arthur," she said to her husband.

She pulled a pale blue envelope from her pocket. "Aunt Dolores wrote me today. She and her friend Howard are planning to visit us in a couple of weeks."

"Hooray!" Mabel yelled. She glanced at Violet.

This would cheer her up, for sure.

Aunt Dolores adored Violet. And Violet adored Aunt Dolores. They hadn't seen her in a while because Aunt Dolores lived far away.

"I want to have a barbeque," her mother said.

"Great idea, honey," her husband replied. "Maybe we can invite our friends and neighbors, too."

"Can we eat corn on the cob? And grilled chicken? And watermelon?" Mabel asked.

"All those things," her mother

promised. "With something else, too. Something special."

"What?" Violet took a step toward her family.

"How about a concert?" their mother said. "Given by Mabel on our new grand piano."

"Yes! Yes! Yes!" Mabel started jumping up and down. "I'll play all Aunt Dolores's favorite songs!"

Violet slumped back into her corner.

"*You'll* get to help with the decorations, Violet," her mother said.

"I don't care."

"And we'll bake a cake for them."

"I don't want to bake a cake."

"This one will be special."

"Oh, yeah?" Violet said, her eyes gleaming. "I'll show you how to make it special."

Chapter Six

In her room, Mabel sat at her desk with pen and paper. She was making a list of songs to play for the concert.

Everyone wanted her to do something different.

Her mother wanted romantic songs.

Her father wanted cheerful songs.

Her piano teacher, Andrea, wanted her to play the most difficult pieces she could.

Violet didn't want her to play the piano at all.

Mabel wondered what Aunt Dolores and Howard wanted. She hoped they weren't fussy.

Her mother told her that Aunt Dolores's

favorite song was "Somewhere Over the Rainbow."

Mabel was trying hard to learn it.

But she couldn't play only one song for the concert. Mabel nibbled on the end of her pen. Then she began to write.

SOME SONGS I CAN PLAY:

1. This Old Man
2. Jingle Bells
3. Ol' Man River
4. Row, Row, Row Your Boat
5. I've Been Working on the Railroad
6. Do Your Ears Hang Low?
7. Yankee Doodle
8. Oh, My Darling Clementine
9. Happy Birthday to You

None of those songs were exactly romantic. And most of them weren't cheerful, either. Except for "Jingle Bells" and "Happy Birthday to You."

Who wanted to hear about snow and

sleigh bells in the middle of summer? And it wasn't anyone's birthday, either.

With a sigh, Mabel went downstairs to practice.

Mabel was in the middle of playing "Somewhere Over the Rainbow."

It was the eleventh or twelfth time she had played it, but Mabel didn't mind.

Andrea always said, "Practice makes perfect," and Mabel wanted the song to be as perfect as possible.

She had just gotten to the part about skies of blue, when she heard someone enter the room.

Mabel tried not to break her concentration. This time, she was going to get the song just right.

Now that she had an audience, Mabel played with extra energy.

Perhaps her mother or father had tiptoed into the room to listen to Mabel play.

Or a neighbor, hearing beautiful music in the sunroom, had crept into the house.

Mabel smiled and glanced at the sheet music again. But it had become blurry and hard to read.

Was something wrong with her eyesight? Did she need glasses?

Mabel blinked. The notes on the page vanished completely.

And then rainbows appeared instead.

"Violet," Mabel said. She turned around.

Her little sister was right behind her. She had a mischievous grin on her face.

"I'm trying to practice," Mabel said.

"Are you playing the rainbow song?" Violet asked.

At her words, rainbows began sliding off the page. They fell onto the keyboard. Some of them slipped between the keys.

Strange sounds floated out of the

piano. They were like nothing that Mabel had ever heard.

"Stop," Mabel said.

"Why?" her little sister replied. "I'm having fun."

A rainbow clung to Violet's wrist. There were musical notes in her hair.

"You're messing up my song. You're messing up my practice. And you're going to mess up Aunt Dolores's concert!"

Violet only shrugged.

"What if you help me?" Mabel offered. "You can turn pages. You can introduce the songs."

Violet shook her head. "I want to play piano. Just like you."

"On the electronic keyboard?"

"The *grand* piano."

"You will, one day," Mabel reassured her. "But you know what Mom said. Wait just a little more, until you're older."

"How long will it take until I'm eight?" asked Violet.

"It'll happen sooner than you think," Mabel said.

"I don't want to wait."

"I understand." She really did. But there was nothing Mabel could do. She wished she could wave a wand and make Violet eight years old.

Not even Violet could do that.

"Please fix this before someone sees it," Mabel said to Violet. She pointed to the rainbows and musical notes. "We don't want to get in trouble."

"Okay, Mabel." Violet snapped her fingers. The rainbows vanished. Musical notes plopped back onto the page.

"That's much better." Mabel hugged her little sister.

Their mother walked in. "What were those horrid sounds?" she asked. "I almost had to stuff cotton in my ears."

"Mabel was practicing," Violet said.

Their mother looked worried. "You're

not going to play like *that* for Aunt Dolores and our friends, are you?"

Mabel sighed deeply. "Don't worry, Mom. I'm going to give them a *great* concert." She turned to the piano and began to play again.

She intended to get it just right this time.

But while she played, she couldn't stop worrying.

What else would Violet try? And how was Mabel going to stop her from using magic again?

She wished that she had a magic help hotline to call.

She wished that she could make a no-magic zone in the piano room.

She wished that Uncle Vartan had been at the door the other night.

She wished she could talk to Uncle Vartan now.

Chapter Seven

Mabel's mother loved throwing parties.

She had invited friends, neighbors, and relatives to the barbeque and concert.

They had packages of rolls. They had cases of soda. They had chicken, hot dogs, and hamburgers. They had watermelons, cookies, cake, and ice cream.

They also had crepe paper streamers and balloons in every color.

"Is Uncle Vartan coming, too?" Mabel asked her mother as they brought groceries into the house.

"Vartan?" Her mother seemed startled. "Coming to the party? I certainly hope not."

"You didn't invite him?" Mabel asked in astonishment. "But he's your little brother. And our uncle. Shouldn't he be here for a family party?"

"It's impossible to get in touch with Vartan," her mother said. "No one ever knows where he is."

Uncle Vartan *did* have a habit of vanishing into thin air. Mabel had seen it herself.

"But he should know about it, at least," Mabel insisted.

Her mother wouldn't meet her eyes. "Who knows what Vartan knows."

"I want him to come!" Mabel cried.

She really wanted Uncle Vartan to hear her play the piano.

She wanted to watch him flip pancakes higher than anyone in the world. She wanted to see his silver rings and his supernatural socks.

And he was the only one who might be able to help her keep Violet under control.

Mabel's mother opened the refrigerator. "Don't hold your breath waiting for Vartan," she warned. "He's unpredictable. A wild card."

"Like Violet?" Mabel asked.

"Violet is *nothing* like Vartan," her mother snapped.

But she *was*, Mabel knew.

Mabel helped her mother put away the rest of the groceries. Then she went into the sunroom to practice again.

Before she practiced, Mabel checked to see where Violet was.

Her little sister was sitting in the sandbox. She seemed to be busy building towers.

"Good," Mabel said to herself. "She's out of the way."

Whenever Mabel sat down at the piano, Violet did something to annoy her.

She played the electronic keyboard very, very loudly.

Or she mixed up Mabel's sheet music.

She also changed the timing on the metronome.

But Violet mostly used magic to interrupt Mabel's practice.

Once she made the piano keys stick together.

When Mabel started to play, she could barely move the keys. It was like she had chewing gum on every finger.

Violet also made the pedals boom like thunder. Lightning and storm clouds had appeared over the piano.

Luckily, she had stopped it before rain started to fall.

And once Violet had flown through the sunroom. Mabel wondered if any other piano players had to deal with *that*.

Probably not even the world's greatest musicians could keep their concentration with Violet zooming through the air.

Mabel couldn't ask her piano teacher what to do about it.

But she could ask Uncle Vartan.

She had already searched through her mother's address book, looking for his number. It wasn't there. There wasn't even an address for him.

Mabel had Googled him, too. There wasn't a trace of him on the Internet. But she was sure she could find him if she just tried hard enough. She was pretty sure she could get him to come to the barbeque, too.

In spite of Violet's best — or maybe worst — efforts, Mabel was determined to make progress.

"Violet, you won't stop me," she said to herself, as she began to play a few warm-up exercises.

"Somewhere Over the Rainbow" was getting better every day.

Mabel had also decided on three other songs: "You Are My Sunshine," "Oh,

What a Beautiful Morning," and "Zip-a-Dee-Doo-Dah."

She was sure that Aunt Dolores would like them. They were all very cheerful songs.

Mabel was in the middle of "On the Sunny Side of the Street." She was playing beautifully. All her practice was paying off.

Onc moment, everything sounded just right.

The next, no sound came from the piano at all.

Mabel blew on her fingers, then tried again. Still nothing.

She glanced out the window.

Violet was pushing over a sand tower.

Mabel tried a third time.

The keys began to make sounds again. But they were like nothing that Mabel had ever heard from a piano.

Each note made a different animal sound. There were moos, meows, caws, chirps, hisses, hoots, roars, and growls.

It wasn't music; it was a jungle or a zoo.

"Twinkle, Twinkle, Little Star" was a cage full of snarling cats.

"Wedding March" twittered and chirped.

"You Are My Sunshine" roared and snorted.

Mabel got up from the bench and leaned out of the window.

"Violet?" she said. "Fix my piano, please."

Violet was filling a pail with sand. "Can't you see that I'm busy, Mabel?"

"If you don't want me to bother you," Mabel said, "then don't bother me."

Violet put down her shovel. "I didn't bother your stupid piano."

"Then why does it sound like an elephant room at the zoo?"

Her little sister snickered.

"I'm losing patience," Mabel snapped.

"Okay, okay." Violet pointed her finger. "Go on, try again."

"It better work."

"It will!" Violet assured her. She trickled sand over her head.

Mabel gritted her teeth. She would never understand her little sister.

"This is the last straw," she warned, as she sat down at the piano again.

Mabel slowly played a few notes, hoping that no growls or roars would spring out at her.

But she heard only music.

If anything, the piano now sounded

better than before. Maybe Violet had given it a tune-up.

Mabel began to play "You Are the Sunshine of My Life."

This time she hit all the notes. She played the song without a single hitch. But she was not happy.

This was *her* concert. It was *her* moment to shine. *She* was the star.

It might be the beginning of a whole new life. One day Mabel would say, "It all started at the barbeque concert."

But Violet wasn't letting up. If anything, she was interfering more and more. She seemed determined to destroy Mabel's dreams.

"I won't let her," Mabel said fiercely to herself.

She had to find Uncle Vartan. Now.

Chapter Eight

That evening, Mabel took out the book that Uncle Vartan had sent to her and Violet.

It was an old-fashioned fairy-tale book with thick, creamy paper; fancy lettering; and pictures that looked real.

It even had its own crimson velvet bookmark.

Mabel kept the book hidden. Or rather, she kept it safe from Violet and her careless ways.

When Violet borrowed Mabel's books, they often came back ripped, stained, smelly, and soaked.

Violet loved the stories in books. But she didn't care about the books themselves.

Even this one.

Mabel loved stories *and* books.

She wasn't going to let anything bad happen to Uncle Vartan's book. It was just too precious.

Every single night, Mabel read a story out of Uncle Vartan's fairy-tale book to Violet before bed.

Still, even after weeks and weeks of reading, she hadn't reached the end of the book.

The book never changed size or shape.

It didn't gain or lose pages.

No one except Mabel ever touched it.

Yet it never, *ever*, ran out of stories.

Mabel had always thought that the book's beauty was magical.

She was beginning to think that the book *itself* was magic.

Now, as Mabel slowly turned the pages, the inscription in the front of the book caught her eye.

"To my dear nieces, Mabel and Violet," Uncle Vartan had written in glittery orange ink. "From your loving uncle."

Mabel frowned. The last time she had looked, it was glittery *silver* ink. And the word *loving* hadn't been there.

When had that changed?

She wondered if Uncle Vartan made secret visits to the book. Did he add stories, change the inscription, or add new pictures?

A chill traveled up Mabel's spine.

Maybe Uncle Vartan could send messages through the book . . .

Or *she* could send messages to *him*.

If she spoke to the book, would he hear?

"Uncle Vartan," she said out loud.

Mabel was glad no one was around. She felt silly talking to a book, even a magical one.

"Are you coming to the barbeque?" Mabel went on. When the book didn't

answer, she added, "You know about it, don't you?"

There was silence. The book didn't so much as rustle its pages.

Perhaps things didn't work like that. The book wasn't a telephone or a computer. Maybe it could only transmit written messages.

Mabel went to her desk and pulled out a blank invitation card.

On the front it read, "You Are Invited To A Party."

On the back it read, "Sparkling Sentiments."

On the inside, there was room to write the address, date, time, and occasion of the party.

Mabel filled everything out. She wrote down all the details of the barbeque. Then she double-checked to make sure she had it right.

As a final touch, she added a personal message.

"Dear Uncle Vartan," she wrote in her favorite navy blue pen, "I hope you can come to the barbeque. I am going to play a concert on the grand piano. Aunt Dolores is going to be there with Howard. Will you come hear me?

"Love, Mabel.

"P.S." she added, "Violet is being a big pest with her magic."

Mabel slipped the card into its envelope. Then she slid it between the pages of the fairy book.

She covered the book with an embroidered cloth and put it back in its hiding place.

She hoped that Uncle Vartan would reply. She had written "RSVP" on the invitation.

The answer came quickly.

As Mabel left her room, a tiny silver feather fluttered down to the floor. She bent down and picked it up.

It had to be from Uncle Vartan. He had received her message.

But what did it mean, Mabel wondered. Was he coming to the party or not?

She stared at the feather for a moment, hoping that it would light up with a yes or a no.

But it just glittered mysteriously in her hand.

She put it in her pocket and hurried downstairs. She was going to tell her mother to buy extra food for the barbeque.

There was a good chance that Uncle Vartan would show up — and he had the biggest appetite of anyone she knew.

Chapter Nine

On the morning of the barbeque, everyone in the house was busy.

Mabel's father was hosing off the patio.

Her mother was hanging crepe paper streamers all over the house.

Her little sister, Violet, was giving her dolls a haircut.

Mabel peeked into her little sister's room. She winced at the clashing colors on the walls.

How did Violet sleep here without getting a headache? Mabel needed sunglasses to enter.

Violet hacked off a clump of hair on her

Sweet Li'l Sarah doll. "How does it look?" she asked.

"Like a tractor mowed her head."

"I'll make it all grow back."

Mabel gave her a serious look. "No magic today, Violet," she said. "You have to promise."

Violet didn't.

She waved her hand over Sweet Li'l Sarah's choppy haircut. Long, silky hair began to tumble down the doll's shoulders.

It reached her waist and then her feet. In a moment, the doll was hidden by a waterfall of hair.

"Hey!" Mabel cried.

Violet picked up her scissors and began to cut the new hair in zigzags. "You are so beee-yooo-tee-full," she sang to her doll.

"Listen to me." Mabel crouched down next to her sister. "This is very important. I'm counting on you. You're a big girl now."

"I am," Violet agreed.

"So *please* don't mess up my concert today," Mabel begged. "*Please* don't do any mischief to my music. And, whatever you do, *no magic*."

"Okay, Mabel," Violet said sweetly as she sheared off hunks of Sweet Li'l Sarah's hair.

"Do you mean it?"

"Of course I do."

Mabel wasn't sure whether to trust her. After all, she was only five years old. And she was Violet.

"If you keep your promise," Mabel said, "we'll do something very special together."

"Take me to the park with you and Simone," Violet said. "Buy me ice cream and play all the games that I like."

Mabel nodded.

"And I want to win at everything. . . ."

"*Violet!*" Mabel said.

"Okay . . . *almost* everything," Violet allowed.

Mabel brushed a few stray doll hairs from her sister's T-shirt. "You won't be sorry," she said.

Mabel went to the piano room to warm up before the concert.

Violet kept her word. She didn't start any mischief. She didn't even come into the room.

The warm-up went well. Mabel was pleased.

"I'm all ready for the concert," she announced to her mother. "Can I help you with anything?"

Her mother pointed to a list. "Here's what's left," she said. "You can see that almost everything is done."

She read the list out loud. "'Take out potato salad, cold drinks, and ice cream at last minute. Bring hamburgers and hot dogs to the grill. Set out rolls. Ring bell to announce concert.'"

"That's it?" Mabel said.

Her mother read the last item on the list. "'Serve cake that I baked with Violet last night.'"

"The cake," Mabel said. She had forgotten about the cake.

"It turned out beautifully," her mother

told her. "There are layers of chocolate and vanilla with hazelnut frosting in between."

"Yum!" Mabel said.

Her mother glanced at the clock. "The guests will be here soon. I'd better fill the cooler with ice."

"And I'd better get dressed." Mabel was still in shorts and a T-shirt.

"You don't have to dress up, honey."

"I want to," Mabel said. It wouldn't be a proper concert if she wore shorts and a T-shirt, even if they matched.

Mabel had picked out a beautiful yellow dress with a pattern of bright red cherries to wear for the concert.

She even had a matching hair ribbon and red sandals to complete the outfit.

"Are you nervous?" her mother asked.

"A little," Mabel admitted. She was more nervous about Violet than anything else.

Her mother gave her a quick smile. "Everyone is going to love hearing you play, Mabel. You've been practicing so hard."

Her mother didn't know how hard it had been, Mabel thought, as she ran up the stairs.

She went into her room and opened the closet door. All her clothes hung in neat, color-coded order.

Except for the party dress.

It wasn't where she had hung it that morning. It wasn't in the closet. It wasn't in her room at all.

Chapter Ten

There was no question in Mabel's mind who was behind the disappearance of her favorite dress.

"Violet!" she yelled.

But Violet had vanished along with the dress.

Mabel wondered what kind of magic Violet had used.

Was it a spell of invisibility? Had she turned the dress into a pile of ashes? Or was it now a red and yellow pair of socks?

Maybe Violet had plucked all the cherries off the dress and eaten them.

In that case, Mabel would find a plain

yellow dress in her closet. But even that wasn't there.

Perhaps Violet hadn't used magic at all. She might have simply hidden the dress in a closet somewhere.

Downstairs, the doorbell rang. The first guests were arriving.

Mabel didn't have time to search for her dress, let alone figure out whether magic was involved or not.

She took a deep breath.

She had always imagined wearing the yellow dress with red cherries while she played.

How could she give the concert without it?

But then, Mabel had prepared for this day for a long time. She knew all the songs practically by heart.

The grand piano was waiting. So were their friends and relatives.

Was she going to quit just because of

a missing dress? Even if it was a very special one?

"No!" Mabel said out loud.

She looked in her closet one more time, just to make sure that the dress was really gone.

It was.

Where was Uncle Vartan when she needed him? Mabel wished that he would appear in a puff of smoke. She wished that he would snap his fingers and restore her dress.

But it was up to her, she realized. She had to go on, with or without him.

"All right, Violet, if that's the way you want it," she said out loud. "Play all your tricks. You can't stop me."

Mabel gritted her teeth. *"I will not let my little sister ruin this concert,"* she vowed.

"Don't you look lovely, dear," said someone's grandmother.

Mabel smiled. She had found a long, sequined, silver dress to wear.

It was nothing like the one that had disappeared. And it wasn't what she imagined wearing.

But it wasn't bad, either. And it fit perfectly.

"So there, Violet," Mabel said silently. She made her way to the piano and watched the guests file in.

"Hey! Mabel!" It was her friend, Simone.

Simone had pointy blue glasses. She had a wide smile. Her teeth were slightly crooked.

Her jaw dropped as she took in Mabel's outfit.

"Silver sequins!" she exclaimed. "And matching silver slippers! And silver rings! Where did you find them?"

Mabel shrugged modestly. "In the costume box."

"Seriously?" Simone said.

"Yes." Mabel herself didn't know why she had looked there. She hadn't expected to find anything. The silver dress was a happy surprise.

"I had to," she went on. "Violet hid my dress."

Simone couldn't stop gaping at her. "You look so different."

"Well, *duh*," Mabel said. "I'm dressed up for the concert."

Simone shook her head. "It's not you."

"It *is* me," Mabel insisted, even though she worried that Simone was right. Third graders didn't wear full-length, silver sequined gowns.

She hoped that she hadn't overdone things. But that was the least of her problems right now.

"Anyway, it's too late to change," she said.

"I guess," Simone said.

"Your dress is *very* glamorous, Mabel," Aunt Dolores said approvingly. She was also glamorous in a lime green sundress with matching straw hat.

"Thanks," Mabel said.

Aunt Dolores put her arm around Mabel's shoulder. "Doesn't she look like a movie star, Howard?"

Howard nodded shyly. He was balding and wore a yellow Hawaiian shirt and baggy shorts.

"I'm so glad you're here," Mabel told them.

Aunt Dolores beamed at Howard. "We're honored," she said. "This is a very special day for us."

"Are you getting married or something?" Simone blurted.

Mabel nudged Simone. Didn't Simone know not to ask such a personal question?

She waited for Aunt Dolores to brush it off. But Aunt Dolores only smiled.

It was almost time to begin. Simone left to find a seat.

Mabel sat down and played a scale or two.

The room was filling up. There was no sign of Uncle Vartan.

Mabel couldn't help feeling a bit disappointed.

But maybe he never received the invitation. After all, she had sent it through a book. Maybe the silver feather was just a coincidence, after all.

Next time, she'd do it the old-fashioned way and use the postal service.

The door opened. Violet came into the room.

Mabel drew in a long breath. Her little sister was wearing a yellow dress with bright red cherries.

It was way too long for her. The dress

drooped over Violet's dirty bare feet. Water and sand stained the skirt.

Mabel wanted to rush over and demand that Violet give her back the dress *right now*.

But their friends and relatives were waiting for her to begin.

As the last few members of the audience took their seats, one final guest slipped in.

"I *do* hope I haven't missed anything," he said to Mabel's mother.

He was wearing a violet seersucker suit with a deep green shirt. Silver cuff links flashed at his wrist.

Mabel's mother turned pale and bit her lip.

Uncle Vartan had arrived.

Too late, Mabel thought. She couldn't get her dress back now. And anyway, she had dealt with it on her own.

She didn't really need him. But she was glad that he was there. She was glad that he had come to hear her play.

Chapter Eleven

"The concert will begin now," Mabel announced in a strong voice.

Then she realized that she had forgotten to plan an introduction.

She didn't know what to say about Aunt Dolores and Howard, "This is a concert for you?" That was kind of awkward.

And she didn't want to say anything about Uncle Vartan, either. That would upset her mother.

And she definitely wasn't going to mention Violet.

"These are all cheerful songs," Mabel said. "For a happy occasion." She hoped that was enough.

She took a deep breath, adjusted her sheet music, and glanced one last time at Uncle Vartan.

He was sitting in the back of the room. His silver cuff links flashed in the sunlight. A leather satchel leaned against his chair.

Was he planning to stay for a while? Mabel hoped so.

Her mother wouldn't like it. There was a deep line between her eyes. Her lips were pressed tightly together.

But Mabel couldn't worry about that now.

She had to worry about getting all the songs right.

And she still had to worry about Violet.

Her little sister was pointing her finger right at Mabel.

Oh no, you don't, Mabel thought. *You're not going to wreck my concert. No way.*

She brought her hands down on the piano keys.

The first chords of "You Are the Sunshine of My Life" floated out.

Mabel didn't miss a single note.

Good work; keep it up, she encouraged herself.

She kept on playing.

But something was different.

It wasn't the music.

It wasn't the piano, either.

It wasn't Mabel.

It was the sunshine. The room was way too bright. And it was getting even brighter.

White-hot, brilliant light poured through the windows. It was as if the sun itself had come into the room.

People blinked and reached for their sunglasses. They held up their hands to shield their eyes.

Mabel wished she had a sunshade. Sweat poured down her face. It hurt to look at the piano keys.

It had to be Violet, of course. But

there was nothing Mabel could do or say now.

Except keep on playing.

She closed her eyes and played the song from memory.

When she finished, everyone broke out in applause.

Mabel wiped her face and began another song.

She didn't look at the audience. She didn't look at Violet. She didn't even look at Uncle Vartan.

She kept on playing.

At the end of the concert, Mabel lifted her hands from the keyboard. She opened her eyes, and let out a long breath.

The blinding light was gone.

She had made it through. And all on her own, without any help from anyone. Even Uncle Vartan. She just knew it.

Violet's magic hadn't stopped her.

Did that mean that Mabel had magic of her own?

She picked up a glass of water and drank it down in one gulp.

The audience applauded wildly.

Chapter Twelve

In the backyard, everyone congratulated Mabel.

"You made us proud," her mother said.

"It was wonderful," her father said. "I loved all the sunshine songs. You lit up the room with your playing."

"Um, yes," Mabel agreed. "I guess you could say that."

"What a concert," Aunt Dolores raved. "I felt as if I was bathed in light."

Howard nodded. "Very special," he agreed.

No one complained about the dazzling light. Maybe it had been worse for Mabel?

She looked around for Violet, but couldn't see her. Where was her little sister now?

And, more importantly, what was she up to?

Simone's eyes gleamed behind her glasses. "What was your trick?" she said. "How did you do it?"

"I practiced a lot," Mabel said.

"I mean, those special effects," Simone said impatiently. "Did you usc a brightening switch?"

Mabel tried to look mysterious, like Aunt Dolores when she was asked nosy personal questions.

But Simone didn't buy it. "Don't play dumb, Mabel." She walked away, annoyed.

"Uh," Mabel said.

Just then, Uncle Vartan stepped forward. "Congratulations," he said to Mabel. "You were stronger than your sister."

"Do I have magic, too?" Mabel asked.

"There are some things that are stronger than magic," Uncle Vartan said.

"Like what?" Mabel demanded.

Uncle Vartan's eyes were pale blue, like the sky on a windy day. They seemed to see everything.

He kissed the top of her head and then turned away.

"Wait a minute!" Mabel said.

Uncle Vartan seemed not to hear her. He hurried toward the door.

Mabel hesitated only a moment.

She dashed through the crowd, ignoring the people who wanted to congratulate her.

"Uncle Vartan!" she called.

Just as he reached the door, she grabbed the coattails of his violet seersucker suit.

He turned around. "You should be proud of yourself," he said. "And now I really have to leave."

He smoothed out his coat and walked through the door.

"Mabel!" Simone cried. "Violet is here. She's wearing your dress!"

"I know." Mabel sighed.

There was a new, oily stain on the dress. She wondered if even magic could get it out.

"And she's very sorry," Simone said. "Aren't you, Violet?"

Violet wouldn't meet her eyes.

"For what?" Mabel asked. There were so many things for Violet to be sorry for. She couldn't even begin to count them.

"For taking your dress," Violet said in a small voice.

Suddenly Mabel felt sorry for her little sister.

Maybe it was because the concert had gone so well. Or because she had been stronger than Violet.

Violet looked so small and unhappy in that huge yellow dress.

Even the cherries looked like measles on her.

"Why did you do it?" Simone scolded Violet. "Mabel had to get a dress from the costume box. Look at her!"

"I don't mind," Mabel said. She liked the silver dress, even if Simone didn't.

Besides, Uncle Vartan had told her she should be proud of herself. She had a strength that even magic couldn't touch.

Violet looked up. "You don't?"

"No," Mabel said. Then she frowned at her little sister. "But you'd better get those stains out. And don't ever try anything like it again!"

Aunt Dolores took Howard's hand and climbed onto the jungle gym. She waved a handkerchief in the air. "I have an announcement."

"I knew it!" Simone cried.

Mabel's mother began to cry.

"Don't worry, Mom," Mabel said. "It's all good."

"I know, honey," her mother sniffled. "I'm crying from happiness."

Mabel looked at her in astonishment. She had never heard of someone crying from happiness.

But it wasn't the strangest thing that had happened today.

"Are you going to be a bride and a broom?" Violet asked Howard and Dolores.

"That's bride and *groom*, Violet," Mabel corrected.

"Yes, we're getting married," Howard said.

Everyone broke into cheers.

"I want you both to be in the wedding," Aunt Dolores said to Mabel and Violet. "Will you be my flower girls?"

"YES!" they said at the same time.

"Will you behave yourself, Violet?" Mabel asked.

Violet nodded. Then she began to sing "Here Comes the Bride" at the top of her lungs.

Mabel rolled her eyes.

Her little sister couldn't stop making mischief. But whatever Violet had in store, Mabel was ready.

About the Author

Anne Mazer is a Mabel who secretly wants to be a Violet. She grew up in a family of writers in upstate New York. She is the author of more than thirty-five books for young readers, including the Scholastic series The Amazing Days of Abby Hayes and the picture book *The Salamander Room.* For more information, please visit Anne at her Web site, www.amazingmazer.com.

Author photo by Mollic Futtcrman

A Little Sister Can Be A Big Pain— Especially If She Has Magical Powers!

Sister Magic
The Trouble with Violet
BY ANNE MAZER
ILLUSTRATIONS BY BILL BROWN
📖 SCHOLASTIC

Sister Magic
Violet Makes a Splash
BY ANNE MAZER
ILLUSTRATIONS BY BILL BROWN
📖 SCHOLASTIC

Sister Magic
Mabel Makes the Grade
BY ANNE MAZER
ILLUSTRATIONS BY BILL BROWN
📖 SCHOLASTIC

Read Them All!

Come flutter by Butterfly Meadow,

the new series by the creators of Rainbow Magic!

Butterfly Meadow #1: Dazzle's First Day
Dazzle is a new butterfly, fresh out of her cocoon. She doesn't know how to fly, and she's all alone! But Butterfly Meadow could be just what Dazzle is looking for.

Butterfly Meadow #2: Twinkle Dives In
Twinkle is feisty, fun, and always up for an adventure. But the nearby pond holds much more excitement than she expected!

SCHOLASTIC
www.scholastic.com

BFLYMEAD1

Meet the fabulous Ruby Marigold Booker!

Think it's hard to stand out when you're the baby sister of the most popular boys on Chill Brook Avenue? Not for Ruby! She sings like nobody's business, has a pet iguana, and dreams of being the most famous animal doctor on the planet!

www.scholastic.com

RUBY

A fairy for every day!

The Rainbow Fairies
Books #1–7

The Weather Fairies
Books #1–7

The Jewel Fairies
Books #1–7

The Pet Fairies
Books #1–7

The Fun Day Fairies
Books #1–7

SCHOLASTIC

www.rainbowmagiconline.com
www.scholastic.com

HiT entertainment

FAIRY2